Empty Pinatas
American Depraved: Book One

Jeffrey Abney

Dedication

To my mother, who always encouraged my writing, and to my grandmother, for introducing me to Stephen King at an incredibly impressionable age.

About the Author

A father of three, a disabled veteran of the United States Army, and a practicing attorney living in St. Louis, Missouri. A lifelong fan of horror and psychological thrillers, and a lifelong aspiring author.

CHAPTER 1 KILL SCENE

The kill had not given him the rush he had anticipated. He had always imagined a surge of endorphins, or perhaps a release of serotonin, would accompany the act. Every movie made the killer out to be the equivalent of a junkie, perpetually on the hunt for his next fix, something akin to a sex addict or a degenerate gambler. That compulsion to feel the excitement of a kill. The mere anticipation of the act driving them to accelerate the rate at which they sought out their victims. The act itself putting them in a never-ending killing cycle from which they could not hope to stop themselves.

He supposed that must all be Hollywood hyperbole.

Instead of that rush, he felt calm. He felt satisfaction. He felt powerful. Hell, he felt virile. He could see himself doing this often, not because of some unrelenting urge driving him to do so, but because he had achieved what he set out to do. It was even easier than he had expected. Tracking them down had been the hard part. But finding them, and then waiting for the right moment to slide a blade into their throat? That was easy.

The blood had come in a spurt at first, then in a thick, dark red wave that narrowly avoided covering his own arm. His victim had collapsed, gurgling and clutching at his throat.

Another thing the movies had gotten wrong: they do not just die right away. They suffer. Their eyes widen in panic, and you can see their mind scramble, either attempting to understand what was happening or perhaps registering that death was near. One thing was certain. They did not want to die. This was an act of taking.

He had frozen at first, watching the blood flow over his victim's hands as the man's fingers clawed at his own throat. But he froze for only a moment.

As wet, gurgling noises filled the air, he placed the knife on the ground gently, almost reverently, before reaching out to the man. He gently but firmly placed both of his black-gloved hands around the man's own hands. The man offered almost no physical resistance as his hands were moved away from his throat. The only noticeable reaction from him was a further widening of the eyes and a slight choking noise emanating from his throat. The blood flowed quicker now that there was no impediment. It took almost no time at all before the man's eyes rolled into the back of his skull. His whole body seemed to go limp as a final gurgle issued from his blood-filled mouth.

The next part he thought he might enjoy. He had gone over it in his head so many times that the act almost seemed like a memory. He had made sure to bring extra-strength trash bags just in case. The last thing he intended was to be caught leaving evidence that he had not planned to.

With a smirk on his face, appearing eager, he picked up the knife from where he had placed it on the ground.

The dead man at his feet had been dressed in a blue, buttoned-up dress shirt. It was clearly tailored and seemed expensive. The shirt was definitely not from some cheap outlet mall. With a slow and deliberate motion, he used the tip of the knife to pop each of the shirt buttons off. Each button made a satisfying *pop* noise as it went flying away.

Once the buttons were completely removed, he started from the bottom and slowly moved the tip of the knife over the exposed undershirt, slow enough to crease the fabric but not tear it. Using his gloved left hand, he grasped the collar of the undershirt and raised it up enough to slide the knife down underneath. Then, with one quick motion, he cut downward, tearing the undershirt in two down the middle.

He suddenly realized this was more intoxicating than he had expected. He had complete control over this body. This corpse. This inanimate piece of flesh.

The smirk on his face blossomed into a full-on grin as that realization came over him.

The last thing he thought before he plunged the knife into the man's stomach was: *I guess the movies weren't complete bullshit after all.*

CHAPTER 2 APRIL 14, 1964

The alarm blared loudly. Cole quickly opened his eyes and blearily made a few feeble attempts to turn off the alarm on his nightstand, slapping at it ineffectively. After the third attempt, he was awake enough to properly smack the button that turned the incessant thing off.

Cole waited for his senses to come to him before throwing back the blankets and starting his morning routine. His bathroom tile was freezing cold to his bare feet as he tiptoed about, turning on his shower, taking a morning piss, and then quickly shaving at his sink. One quick shower, a dash of deodorant, and a brushing of teeth later, and he was ready to throw on one of his half-dozen, similar-looking dark gray suits and whatever tie happened to be closest to the front of his tie rack.

Special Agent Cole Hunter was born in St. Louis, Missouri, on November 3, 1942. While attending high school, he discovered an interest in psychology. He had always been a curious child. Once he focused that curiosity towards learning what motivated people to do what they did, he knew that he wanted to spend his life in pursuit of that knowledge. The son of a local sheriff, Cole was also raised with a distinct notion of right and wrong. He had been instilled with a firm sense of what he believed justice looked like.

In the winter of 1964, he had been selected to begin training at the FBI National Academy. Ten weeks of training later, he had been lucky enough to be assigned to his hometown. The St. Louis Division Field Office of the Federal Bureau of Investigation had been re-established in 1924 after a brief shutdown in 1920. By the start of 1964, its primary focus was local organized crime and the increasing number of civil rights cases. It seems organized crime was getting the best of the local cops—but the local cops were getting the best of anyone who wasn't lucky enough to be born white.

Cole had worked his whole life towards today. Countless hours studying in college to earn a dual degree in psychology and criminalistic studies, while finishing top of his class at Saint Louis University. This had taken a great deal of discipline on his part, and the sacrifice had been his private life. He had forgone any meaningful personal relationships while grinding through the dual degree program and had even allowed ties to his family to become strained in his single-minded pursuit. However, getting accepted into the FBI training program on his first try had made it all worthwhile in his mind. This was the achievement he had been working his whole life towards, topped only by the day he graduated from the FBI National Academy.

His goal throughout the academy had been to be stationed near his home, so he could make a difference in the lives of those he knew and loved. He had clearly kissed the right asses—or someone had decided that his knowledge of the area would be useful—because he got his wish. When he received notice that he was to be assigned to the St. Louis Field Office, he was as happy as he could ever remember being. Now, today was his first day as an actual FBI Special Agent, and the first day working in the field office for his home city. He rushed out the front door and hurriedly flew down the four steps that led from his front porch to the walkway heading towards his car.

His dad had purchased him a 1958 Buick Model 41 convertible when he graduated high school, four years prior. It had a cream-colored exterior and white interior with a black rag top. It was Cole's favorite possession, without question. He quickly got into the front seat, put the top down, and began backing out of his driveway.

This was the bicentennial of St. Louis. The multiple celebrations planned throughout the spring and summer would bring with them numerous out-of-town criminals, would create opportunities for altercations and crimes that would not normally occur, and—hopefully—would provide Cole with a busy first few months as an agent.

As he flew down the side streets, he wondered what exciting cases he might be assigned to. With the top down, he was enjoying the fact that the St. Louis weather finally seemed to be shaking off the remnants of winter and fully embracing spring. He was hoping for a juicy bank robbery case or one where a mobster was shaking down the local unions.

The Field Office was just off Market Street and home to ten Special Agents, supported by five secretaries. The office was located within walking distance of Busch Stadium in the downtown area. Today was the start of the Cardinals' baseball season. All the buzz around town was that the team was slow and lacking leadership after the heart and soul of their squad for 22 years, Stan Musial, had retired. It had been 18 years since the Redbirds had won a pennant, and that streak did not appear to be in any danger of being broken any time soon.

Cole quickly found a parking spot and slid his car between the lines in one fluid motion. Parking in St. Louis was a nightmare, so he took finding a spot so easily as a good sign of how the day was going to go. With a smile on his face and barely contained excitement in his step, he hopped out of his car and strode towards the door of the field office to start his first day as an FBI Agent.

CHAPTER 3 SPECIAL AGENT

The first thing Cole noticed as he walked through the doors was the thick cloud of cigarette smoke that seemed to hover in the air like it was a permanent atmospheric fixture in the office.

The front doors were guarded by a portly gentleman wearing a security guard's outfit, fully equipped with a revolver on his hip and a glare upon his face. Cole pulled out his credentials and flashed them at the guard, expecting some official act or even a slight bit of interest. Instead, he received a barely audible grunt from the guard and a head nod directing him to proceed.

Cole proceeded past the guard and looked at the office. The office was an open area with rows of ten desks arranged evenly on each side of the room. Each desk had a name plate for a special agent, and after perusing the rows, Cole found his name plate on the desk nearest the bathroom door.

The back of the room was home to a sizeable office window that had the blinds closed. The door to that office read 'Director Shehbazski' and had an ancient secretary stationed at a desk outside of it.

Cole walked towards the ancient secretary, past the rows of desks, most of which were occupied with suited men smoking and reviewing various papers. Each man sported varying degrees of annoyed looks on their faces. As he approached the ancient secretary, whose desk plate says Opal *Huskey,* she stopped typing, looked up at him, and raised an eyebrow as she scanned him over.

"You must be Special Agent Hunter. Mr. Shehbazski is in his office and waiting for you. It being your first day, he expected you to be here fifteen minutes ago."

Cole blushed. "I… I… was told to be here at eight. Is he angry?"

Opal got up from her desk, quicker than one would expect for a woman of her age, and walked to the office door. As she opened it, she said, "I guess there's only one way to find out. In you go."

Cole nodded his head and hurriedly walked through the office door.

As he entered, he noted that the office was very utilitarian, lacking almost any decoration or personal effect on display. The only notable decoration was a framed award that was unfamiliar to Cole. It read 'FOR OUTSTANDING SERVICE ANGLO-IRAQI 1940-1941' and then listed Shehbazski as the recipient.

"I see you have noticed my commendation."

Startled, Cole looked down to see a man, roughly in his late 50s with the bushiest eyebrows he had ever seen, sitting and writing at the only desk in the office.

"I got that during the German invasion of Russia in June of 1941. I was part of a clandestine unit responsible for the disruption of supply lines to Russia whilst simultaneously making it look like the Nazis were responsible. The secondary goal was the destabilization of the Iraqi monarchy. This directly led to the monarchy's collapse in 1958."

Cole did not really know how to respond to that. "That's great, sir. Um… I am Cole Hunter, your newest agent."

Director Shehbazski raised one bushy eyebrow and sighed. "No shit, Agent Hunter. As much as I am looking to get to know all the exciting things that make you tick, I need you on scene."

Cole immediately straightened up. "Already, sir? I mean, yes, sir. What type of scene?"

Director Shehbazski's piercing eyes looked Cole slowly up and down before he sighed again.

"The local police have requested our presence at a murder scene. At this stage, it is consultation only. We have a tenuous relationship with St. Louis's finest, at best. They hate us poking around their cases and accuse us of stealing their busts. So, this is a big deal that they are asking for our help."

"I understand, sir. Did they give any specifics about the murder?"

Cole withdrew a pocket-sized notepad and pen from his inner breast pocket.

"I suspect your partner will fill you in when you get there. All we were told is that it was gruesome. So, if you haven't eaten breakfast yet, I wouldn't recommend doing so before you head over there. Opal will give you the address of the scene where you will meet up with Special Agent Johnson, who is already there. Johnson isn't particularly happy he is being partnered with someone fresh out of training, so you better hurry your ass up and not keep him waiting."

With that, the Director put his head back down and began to write again.

Cole, having been summarily dismissed, turned and walked out of the office as quietly as possible.

As he passed by Opal's desk, she had her hand raised with a slip of paper in it, which he grabbed before heading towards the front door.

CHAPTER 4 VICTIM #1

Cole was surprised at how easy it was to find parking in the area of St. Louis known as The Hill. The crime scene was an alley behind an Italian restaurant called Dominic's. The restaurant had been open less than three months and was rumored to be owned by a John Vitale, or Johnny V, to his associates. Johnny V was a known underboss for the Mafia in St. Louis, which was headed by Anthony Giordano, aka Tony G.

After Cole parked his car, he walked behind the restaurant and flashed his badge at the two uniformed police officers guarding the perimeter.

"I am looking for Special Agent Johnson."

The first officer turned to the second officer and said, "I got your Special Johnson, pal." Both officers then proceeded to chuckle, causing Cole to look at them both disapprovingly.

From beyond the police tape line, Cole heard someone call out, "It's about time you got here. Quit cracking jokes with the local baton lickers and get your ass over here."

Cole looked past the two cops to see a man in a black suit with a black tie, roughly in his mid-forties and puffing on a cigar. He appeared as strait-laced as they came, at first look. Cole ducked under the police tape, passed the two laughing cops, and headed towards his new partner.

Cole reached out his hand as he approached him. "Special Agent Johnson?"

With a squint and a grimace directed towards Cole's outstretched hand, Johnson replied, "Just Johnson, kid. Now, don't embarrass me and try not to get acne cream all over the crime scene. Your only job here is to observe, do you understand? Just observe."

Cole put his hand back down to his side and nodded towards Johnson in understanding. Johnson grunted, turned, gruffly said, "Follow," and walked down the alley.

Cole checked his watch, then the corpse. Johnson squatted nearby, silent, tracing the butchered man's outline with a latex-gloved finger.

The medical examiner, Dr. Petrovic, muttered to herself in thickly accented English, dabbing at her forehead with a cotton handkerchief. Hunter hovered close, peering at the man's face: blue lips, waxen skin, a jaw etched with five o'clock shadow. He couldn't have been dead more than twelve hours.

There were no visible wounds apart from the thick sailor's stitches that ran from throat to groin, a botched attempt at needlework slackening now with heat. No blood, not even on the concrete where the victim hung above a halved metal barrel. The killer had bled him elsewhere.

Petrovic cut away the stitches with a small surgical blade. Cole stiffened, blinking twice, while Johnson said, "Kid is getting his feet wet the hard way. What do we got, doc?"

The cavity gaped open, nothing inside but darkness and a hollow echo.

The medical examiner said, "Heart's gone. Lungs, liver, lower GI. This was surgical. Whoever did this knew what they were doing."

She reached down with tweezers and pulled out three small lengths of hair.

"If we get any suspects, we can at least run these to get a match."

She gently placed them in a plastic bag and sealed them shut.

"Well, ball's in our court now," Johnson said, grinding a finished cigarette against the outer wall of the building. The cigarette butt squelched in the mush of its predecessors, and he immediately put another one between his fingers and lit up again.

"My guess is he crossed someone, and they took it personally."

Cole looked at the body in confusion.

"You don't think it's mob-related? We are in their territory, right? Couldn't this be some sort of message?"

Johnson absentmindedly kicked at the pile of cigarette butts.

"A few years ago, Tony G took over this area with his underboss, Johnny V. They have left more than a few bodies all over the city, but nothing like this. This… I don't know what this is. We should kick it back to the local cops."

"Shouldn't we work it until we know for sure it isn't the mob? What if it *is*, and we waste valuable days letting another agency work this case, messing it up?"

Johnson sighed and looked up from the pile of cigarettes directly at Cole.

"Fine, kid. But we are kicking this the first chance we get, and I am not babysitting you on this. You are doing the legwork."

Cole smugly smiled in victory immediately before a flash temporarily blinded him.

Johnson went running down the alley, yelling at a reporter holding a camera, but the reporter was too quick and got away.

CHAPTER 5 APRIL 28, 1964

He had been anticipating this all week.

The second victim was an improvement even before the work began. No hesitation, no trembling nerves, and by the time he had the body strung up, inverted and swaying gently like a freshly gutted deer, he had felt a radiant, wild satisfaction. The setup had gone smoother than expected, removal of the organs had been more efficient, and just the little experience from before had taught him the importance of preparation.

The pleasure wasn't in the logistics, though; it was in the moment of the kill itself. His first kill had been curiosity-driven and meant to quiet an all-encompassing urge. This kill was crisp and clinical at first. He had envisioned it in advance. Only once the life bled from the victim did a deepening indulgence set in. Only once the blood was pouring down his hands did he let himself sink into the ecstasy of the whole thing.

This one died less quickly because he took his time. He was careful, and was able to note the victim's body spasming, the gradual slackening of muscle, and the slowing of the arterial blood flowing from the incisions. After, while the body began to cool, he worked his gloved hands with precision, making incisions so perfect it seemed less like violence and more like art. Each insertion of the blade popping beneath the thin resistance of skin. Each meticulous slice exposing the warm, coppery emergence of the organs hidden below.

In a sense, he began to feel a companionship with this victim.

No… not a companionship, that was too romantic. It was more like a sense of ownership of this individual. The feeling of companionship was more attuned to this victim's anatomy. The heart, the liver, the ever-unwinding loops of intestine, all so efficiently separated and so thoroughly possessed. He took his time removing each delicate organ and placing them in their new containers. The lungs were heavier than expected, and he enjoyed hefting each in turn before arranging them in a careful row, as if for an audience. The trick was to keep the aesthetic: no spillage, no mess. The arrangement must satisfy an internal symmetry, or the kill would begin to lessen its satisfaction.

Afterwards, he stood for a moment, the air tasting thick with bleach and offal, and reflected on the improvement. Each repetition had revealed what could be refined. He was learning not just technique, but taste. The removal of each organ, the gentle weaving of the thick black thread through the cooling flesh, and the detailed cleaning of each surface afterwards, brought greater pleasure than at first imagined.

It made him long to redo his first kill.

He looked over his work, the victim now a hollowed-out chrysalis, and considered what would come next. This was no ordinary urge. It was a calling to perfect something. To leave a mark that could not be misconstrued, even by men paid to misunderstand.

The message was clear to him: an escalation of craft and intent is required.

The authorities would find the body soon enough. But why not control the timing? This is his narrative creation, is it not? Sending the authorities a token of this night would get them moving on *his* timeline. Sending a token to help their investigation—and a little something to demonstrate the level of sophistication they are unwittingly up against.

CHAPTER 6 VICTIM #2

The morning came early and found Johnson slouched at his desk, the early edition folded on the blotter before him. *"Killer Drains Victim Like Blood Sausage,"* the sub-header screamed, and below that, a blurry photograph of the alley behind Dominic's—the silhouette of the body swinging gently among the steam from the kitchen vents.

Johnson ran a thumbnail along the edge of his teeth and spat a tiny crescent of cuticle into the wastebasket. He didn't need to read the article; the hacks in town always got their facts from the uniforms first, and the cops resented the Feds, so almost nothing was left out. The paper had a way of demonizing the authorities. Johnson thought that maybe it was their own way of coping with the never-ending string of atrocities that time and again wound through St. Louis like the brown water of the Mississippi.

The only good thing the cops did was to run down who the victim was.

The body of the victim had been identified as one Andrew Spethanopolous—a local, middle-class, Republican family man who was nearing retirement age. The only lead they had, other than the hair found at the scene, was a witness who had informed the police they had seen the victim in a heated argument at the bar the week before.

Apparently, Mr. Spethanopolous's son-in-law had taken to beating on his daughter, and the two had gotten heated over it. Unfortunately, when Cole called on the wife to confirm this, she had done so quickly, but she had also given her husband an alibi for the night of the murder. They had apparently been together all evening, and she had described her husband as "incapable of having the balls to try and kill her father."

With the only tangible lead fizzling out, Johnson was left to read the paper, while Cole was educating himself by reviewing the rap sheets of the local mafia members.

One of the receptionists walked through the front door and made a beeline to Cole's desk, where she deposited a package wrapped in brown paper.

Cole raised a questioning eyebrow at the woman, and she said, "It was hand-delivered, and it has your name on it. That's all I know."

Cole shook the box a little and could hear the jostling inside of something firm, but not entirely solid.

"Maybe it's a fruitcake?" he said as he pulled out a letter opener and cut the seal of the package.

As soon as the package flaps opened up, a sweet, meaty funk wafted out, and blood-red smears could be seen on the undersides of the flaps. Cole reactively shoved the box away from himself so quickly you could hear something inside had shifted and sloshed.

Johnson got up from his desk and slowly walked over to the package. When he looked down, he pulled out a white card and read aloud:

"If you wrong me, am I not allowed to right that wrong? If you fleece me, am I not allowed to recoup my losses? If you break a vow against me, am I not allowed to see us part?"

Johnson turned the card over. "You're not going to believe this. There's an address on the card. Wanda, can you get this down to evidence, please?"

Wanda nodded reluctantly and walked towards the box. What she saw inside was a bloody, congealed mess that looked like skinless snakes.

Johnson motioned for Cole.

"Wanda, tell the boys they are intestines, and we think it is from the Spethanopolous case. Oh, and have the local police send us some backup."

Wanda immediately held her mouth as if to stop from vomiting and pulled away from the package.

"Kid, do you still think this is mobsters?"

*****

By the time the agents got to the address on the card, the local police were already on scene. The address was located in an area of St. Louis called The Hill, and the majority of the police and fire department had chosen to buy their homes there.

The police had already kicked in the front door as the two agents were getting out of their car.

When they walked through the front door, they found a man dangling from the ceiling and sewn up like the original victim. Not a drop of blood was evident, and Johnson noticed that, for the first time that week, he had nothing to ask the uniforms to back away from. He just yelled for somebody to get forensics, and all that could be heard was someone else puking next to a cruiser.

Johnson stepped outside. The city's swelter pressed against his shirt like a hand. The smell was worse than the last one. There was no mistake—this was the same guy who did the first one. He had a very distinct signature that, despite being in the heart of mob territory, was clearly the work of one man.

Cole came walking out behind Johnson with something in his hand.

"We may have gotten lucky. There was a ledger found in the front room. Looks like this belongs to a bookie. Maybe our killer or their enforcer?"

Johnson sighed.

"Kid, this would be a hell of a way to send a message. Think of the repeat business. We are more likely to find that the ledger belongs to the man who is currently strung up inside."

The medical examiner was soon on the scene and confirmed the man was missing all of his organs—exactly like the first victim. A canvas of the area revealed the man's name was Gianni Colombo, and he was the local bookmaker, which all but confirmed whom the ledger belonged to.

CHAPTER 7 THE SUSPECT

Johnson skimmed the two-column headline, tongue stuck to his molars by dried coffee. It wasn't even nine, and already the *Post-Dispatch* had gotten creative: *El Pinatero Taunts City, Claims Fourth Victim.* The article ran beside a line drawing of a donkey-shaped piñata with cartoonish XXs over the eyes, which seemed, to Johnson, both tasteless and apt.

He'd always found St. Louis prone to macabre humor—something about murder in the shadow of the Arch lent itself to bad puns and worse sketches.

He read the story twice, jaw setting tighter each time. The details were accurate enough, which suggested either a leak or a reporter with an appetite for dumpster-diving behind the station. Johnson preferred the latter; at least a stray reporter could be run off by a badge and a mean look, while a leaker was a rot that never quite healed.

Fat chance of a mean look doing anything, now.

The telephone on Cole's desk rang, and Cole immediately picked the receiver up and eagerly answered. Johnson continued to read the article for a third time but stopped when he looked up and saw the expression on Cole's face grow serious.

"We got a tip that came through the wire. The word on the street is that someone with the initials *P.A.* owed Gianni a lot of money, and we should be able to find his address next to his initials in the ledger. Do you have that ledger over by you?" Cole asked Johnson as he set the receiver back in its cradle, hand clammy against the black surface.

Johnson put his paper down, pulled open a drawer on his desk, and retrieved the leather ledger they had found at the crime scene. After a few minutes of rifling through the pages and columns,

Johnson found *Patsy's* initials and saw a huge figure written next to his name in the next column—underlined twice in red ink.

Johnson raised an eyebrow and looked up at Cole.

"We know this guy. We were just at his house."

Cole's eyes widened as it dawned on him that they may have let the killer go—and allowed him to kill again.

"I'll drive," Cole said, as they both got up quickly from their desks and headed towards the door.

CHAPTER 8 VICTIM #3

Patsy blinked against the daylight when they cut him loose, the two Bureau men walking him back out through the waiting room in reverse order, like the tape had rewound. It was almost six when the Feds released him, and he stood on the steps of the field office, watching a summer drizzle lacquer the pavement.

The older one, Johnson, gave him a dry, almost respectful smirk—as if to warn, you're free, but only because we're letting you. The younger agent, the one with the haircut that belonged at West Point and not in a city with river mud for blood, had kept his eyes on his folder, flipping the pages like he was already fitting *Patsy* for prison clothes.

"We'll be in touch if we need anything else, Mr. Patsy," he said. Patsy almost laughed.

They had been at him for hours, and he had kept giving them the same responses.

"Yes, I owed some money."

"No, I didn't kill my father-in-law."

"I was with my wife both nights."

They only stopped when he finally agreed to give them a hair sample to test against the one they had found at the crime scene.

His jaw ached from hours of clenching. He thumbed the canary-yellow lighter in his pocket—the same one they'd eyed and catalogued. They couldn't pin anything on him, but *Patsy* knew the game wasn't over.

He stretched his arms and neck, wincing at the static in his nerves, and started home. His ride was gone, so he walked, cutting through alleys as the light failed and the city's neon turned on, smeared by the rain.

By the time he hit Cherokee Street, his shirt collar was stuck to his neck, and the whole area reeked of wet cardboard, fried onions from the taqueria, and the warm rot of a dead bird wedged somewhere nearby.

He walked through his front door, exhausted, and went immediately up to his bed. He was asleep before his head even hit the pillow.

He didn't notice there were two plain-clothed police officers in a dull Ford across the street, pretending to read newspapers or adjust the radio—but mostly just looking at his house.

*****

No one would let him see the body. They locked him in a room off the kitchen, handcuffed to the radiator with a length of cold steel biting into his wrist.

The first cop had barely managed to drag *Patsy* off the tile before he upchucked bile all over the cop's shoes, then collapsed into himself—fists balled, knees drawn up to his chest—while someone phoned it in and another shuffled around frantically, searching himself for handcuffs destined for immediate use.

Neither of them could look him in the face. They kept glancing at the pools of blood forming around the edge of the linoleum, the blood seeping slowly but surely into the seams. Neither of them wanted to look into the bathtub more than once.

After cuffing him, the younger of the cops gagged, hand clamped over his mouth, nausea riding up from his gut as he stumbled backwards out of the bathroom, the coppery stench like a bucket over his head. The stench was a wall.

Warm metal. Piss. Sweetly rotten chicken-skin odor.

The hallway light picked out streaks of diluted blood trailing from the bathroom, and the blurred reflection of the scene painted

22

red across the lacquered floor. Downstairs, he eventually heard the echo of radios, the front door banging open, and the thud of boots.

He pushed himself off the wall and tried to say something to the detectives that arrived, but his voice snagged onto the memory of the bathtub—the neat saw lines where the woman's torso used to be.

When *Patsy* had first walked into the bathroom, he tottered, hand catching the doorframe, watching the pink water lap around Linda's knees. The organs floated like toy boats.

At first, his mind wouldn't let him see her face. He clocked her dress—turquoise, the one she wore for New Year's Eve at Uncle Gino's—and the wet brown hair stringing over her chin, but the head was all wrong. Too wide. The mouth stretched and caved in. It was as if someone had tried to make a Linda mask out of wax and jammed it on a pumpkin.

The mouth looked unnatural, like something had been placed into it.

He had taken three steps onto the linoleum, knees knocking, and dropped hard in front of the tub. The skin on her hands was rubbery, too pale even for someone dead this long. He had touched her wrist. Still warm, somehow.

He had squinted, trying to see past the ruined mess of her belly, and his vision swam. He did not know how long he had been on his knees next to her, and the only thought in his head was that he wished someone would stop with all that screaming so he could focus.

It took the cops arriving before he realised he was the one who was doing all the screaming.

*****

No one believed *Patsy* when he said he did not kill his wife, his father-in-law, or his bookie. In his wife's mouth, the coroner found her father's missing heart, and within all that bathtub viscera, the bookie's spleen had been found.

A thorough search of the house uncovered a receipt for a storage unit three blocks away. Cole and Johnson immediately got a warrant and found there was a refrigerated storage unit in *Patsy's* name. Inside the unit, the first thing that hit them was the odor of old blood—in that sharp, animal way—thickening the air like butcher's tar.

They took a crowbar to the unit's lock and immediately discovered glass jars full of dry brown residue that was obviously blood, and various organs that had begun to look leathery and warped from slow decomposition. Each jar sat on a standing deep flowerbed that was filled to the brim with ice instead of soil.

Johnson: "I bet you twenty that the blood types will come back for the first two victims."

Cole, shaking his head: "I may be new, but I'm not taking a sucker's bet."

Patsy was immediately arrested for all three murders, and the bloody jars came back as matching the blood types of the first two victims. The lab also finally returned the results from the hair sample found at the first crime scene—and it was a perfect match for *Patsy*.

The look on *Patsy's* face when Johnson showed him the lab report wasn't what stuck with him. It was the look on Johnson's face when they showed *Patsy* the lab report. The agent was waiting for a crack—expecting the bottom to fall out, or for *Patsy* to break down in a squall of hiccupping confessions. But *Patsy* never confessed or cracked. He just looked defeated.

There was nothing left in him to break. The world had played all its cards, and here he was, holding a fistful of bad hands, waiting for the dealer to take his wedding ring and the last slugs from his chest.

Maybe that's why, when they read out the evidence and said, "Her blood was under your nails, your hair was on her father's body, and the blood in your storage unit was type-matched to the bookie and her father," *Patsy* just went slack and felt a hollow expand inside him like a second set of ribs.

CHAPTER 9 TRIAL

Patsy didn't fight at first. Not the way a TV man would. They led him to his cell after the verdict, right past the *Post-Dispatch* boys with their cigarettes and slicked-back hair, and he barely squared his shoulders.

The air in the holding cell was so thick with bleach and old urine it burned his nostrils.

"Gonna make the chair shine for you," the guard said, too loud for the short hallway, and the old anger raked down Patsy's spine—hot, and then immediately hollow.

They took his shoes, belt, and the drawstring from his slacks, but left him his St. Christopher medal. Maybe they thought it was a joke.

He could still taste the sweat of the courtroom, the rusty tang of his own shirt collar where the bailiff had grabbed him, hard enough to pop the third button. The whole time, the Yankee college lawyer slouched next to him, scribbling with a green pencil, never looking him in the eye.

In the months between the verdict and the day they carted him off to Bonne Terre, *Patsy* heard from no one but his public defender and an affable priest who smelled like bug spray and caramels.

His mother wrote, once, telling him to "offer up suffering for the souls in purgatory." He remembered her hands—twisted and blue about the knuckles—and the way she broke bread by slapping it hard against the table edge. She'd loved him, he supposed.

They kept his cell icebox cold. The light cut through the slit in the door and ran a weak line over his cot. He found himself watching that line all hours, charting the tiny hairs and dead skin flakes that shimmered there. Sometimes he saw—he thought he saw—a moth battering its wings in the line, always failing to cross.

Nights were worse.

The trial was a blur to him. The evidence had been irrefutable, according to the prosecutor. His hair matched the hair found at the first crime scene. He had motive to kill the first victim. The storage unit was in his name. The man who ran the storage unit somehow managed to pick him out of a line-up. Also, he had owed victim two a lot of money, and all the blood in the storage unit came back as a match for both the first two victims.

That he was covered in his wife's blood, and was found next to the body, was all the evidence needed to convince the jury of his guilt in her death.

The Jury took just one hour to convict him on all three counts of first-degree murder. There were numerous lesser charges he was also found guilty of, but *Patsy* never really understood what the point of charging him with improper disposal of a body would do that a murder charge wouldn't.

When his public defender asked if he wanted to appeal, all he said was, "What's the point?"

After the sentencing, they delivered him to Death Row. He catalogued each moment with the grim clarity of someone whose life had been whittled down to the purity of seconds and square inches.

The cell was nothing—less, even—a fat blue-walled joke with a cot, a steel toilet, and bars so cold they bit through skin if you napped your head against them.

At first, he stuck to the old routine—push-ups, wall sits, sharpening the edges of his thumbnail with that tiny slip of cement—because habits were the last thing no one could take from him.

EPILOGUE OCTOBER 15, 1964

[Patsy] sits alone in his cell. The cell is dark, with only one slit window casting light into it. The light is shadow-thatched due to the steel mesh bars affixed to the window exterior. The cell itself has a solid steel sink, a filthy toilet, and a single steel cot with a dirty and stained mattress resting atop it. On that mattress, *[Patsy]* sits with his head in his hands. He wears a dingy gray prison jumpsuit that looks almost too big for his body.

The metal clank of a bolt echoes through the room as the solid cell door is unbolted and slid to the right, revealing bars still in place to separate the cell from the rest of the prison.

A disgusted-looking prison guard barks into the cell, "It's time for your confession, you piece of shit. Though, I'm not sure what good it'll do you. Repentance requires you to actually feel bad for what you did. Absolution's not for you, or for where you're going after they gas your ass tonight.

"Now play nice with the priest, because if I hear any sign of distress from him, I'm coming in here to make sure you head into the next life with as many broken ribs as I can manage."

With that, the guard glowered at the prisoner before stepping out of view.

In the guard's place sat a priest, dressed in full Last Rites apparel. With a firm and calming voice, the priest began to speak.

"*[Patsy]*, I am here to give you your last rites, and I ask that you repent your sins to God before your soul leaves this mortal realm and you are forced to bathe in the lake of fire in Hell for all eternity.

"*[Patsy]*, will you please tell me your sins so that I may unburden your soul, and God can allow you to walk through the gates of Heaven, washed clean of the taint you brought on this world?"

Patsy raised his head from his hands, exposing his tear-soaked cheeks and noticeably red and wet eyes.

"Father, I've not been a perfect man. My heart has been full of anger and pride. I've stolen from people. I've cheated. I admit to that. I've not always done the right thing, but God knows I did *not* kill those three men! I am not a monster, and I will not ask for forgiveness for another man's sins."

His head fell into his hands again as he began to weep once more. Through muffled tears:

"You have to believe me, Father!"

The priest leaned forward and spoke low and slow.

"What is a monster, my son? Is it the man who beats his wife, or is it the man who kills his father-in-law when confronted about hurting his daughter? Is it the degenerate gambler, or the man who kills the bookie when he gets in too deep? Or is it the man who kills his own wife?

"Maybe it is not for me to say what a monster is. But all three of those people lost their lives because of *you*, my son. Don't you think you should at least admit to God that you played a significant part in their deaths?"

Patsy's head came up slowly and his face turned red with anger as he screamed:

"I PLAYED NO PART IN THEIR DEATHS!!!!!"

"*Patsy. Patsy.* Be honest with yourself. You think you played no part in their deaths?

"You can take me for a fool, but please don't take God for a fool. He knows your sins. He knows what's in your heart. He knows the hand you played in their deaths—even if it wasn't by your own hands, directly. You set off the chain of events that led to their deaths. That is undeniable."

Patsy's mouth untightened, and his eyes widened slowly. "What do you mean, 'even if it was not by my own hands?'"

A crooked and malicious grin spread across the priest's face, slowly, as he began a low and deep chuckle.

"You don't remember me, do you? Do you remember Cherokee Street about a year ago? Well, maybe a year and a few days now. Do you remember hitting someone on the back of the head with your gun, kicking them in the ribs repeatedly, and then stealing their wallet while they were facedown in the mud?"

Patsy's eyes widened even further as memory flooded back to him. The priest leaned in even closer to speak.

"I bet you thought the rain would keep me from getting a good look at you. I bet you thought the kicks to my ribs and the shot to my head would keep me from following you three blocks to where you'd parked your car. The irony is that the rain you hoped would conceal your assault helped me follow you—to ascertain your identity."

The priest scooted his chair closer to the cell bars, the metal chair legs screeching across the concrete.

"After you robbed me, humiliated me, and left me in the mud, I was possessed by a certain feeling of rage. A fiery burning that I just could not let go. But I'll admit that I didn't try too hard. I liked this rage. It was fuel. It allowed me to track down your home, where I saw that one of your hobbies—besides mugging strangers—was beating on your pretty bride."

"It was a simple matter for me to find out who her father was and where he liked to drink. It was an even simpler matter to find out when you'd be at the bar together and let it slip that his little girl was being treated unkindly."

"What was a little more complicated was finding a good time to kill Mr. Spethanopolous. Lucky for me, you're a creature of habit, and you always placed bets with Gianni the night before a big game. You sure do love your Cardinals, don't you?"

"Since I had your schedule down, I broke into your home and took some of your hair from the comb in your bathroom. Once I left that at the crime scene, your days were numbered."

Patsy's face turned white with disgust as he listened to the priest recount how he had framed him. The priest's smile continued to grow as he explained further.

"Did you know that no one in this city checks identification for anything? It's really not smart. But it does allow someone the freedom to rent a refrigerated storage unit in anyone's name without many questions."

"Would you believe that all it took for me to copy your appearance was a hat, a fake moustache, and a coat? The old man at the counter would probably have picked any moustached man out of a line-up."

The priest chuckled.

"The cops really did me a favor there. Who does a line-up with five moustache-less men and one with a moustache?"

"After that, it was just a matter of leaving Mr. Spethanopolous's organs about. I bet you were probably relieved when you heard that Gianni had been killed. That debt wiped out?"

"Did you know *I* wasn't the one who tipped the cops off to that? Your aggrieved wife took it upon herself to drop a letter to the police. Gianni's ledger only had your initials next to the debt owed. Her letter tied you directly to him, and you already had a direct connection to Spethanopolous."

"There was probably no need to continue. The law would have been able to do their job well enough to arrest you. But I had to complete your punishment. You understand that, right? You understand that now, don't you?"

Through gritted teeth: "You had to lose everything, *Patsy*. And that is exactly what I took from you. When I left your dead wife swimming in a bathtub of viscera and organs for you to find, I had a smile on my face."

"I took great pleasure placing her own father's heart into her mouth, because I wanted *you* to see it first. Is that what you saw first? I've been dying to know. Tell me if that's the first thing you saw."

Patsy aggressively leapt up from the mattress and threw himself towards the prison bars, screaming in rage:

"FUCK YOU!!! YOU FUCKING SICK FUCK!!!!!"

The prison guard hurriedly stormed down the hall towards the cell. The priest gave *Patsy* a quick smile, then threw himself back away from the bars and gave the guard a look of faux fear and panic.

The guard: "Get out of here, Padre. I think this lost cause just earned himself a lesson in manners."

The priest just nodded and began to leave. He couldn't resist giving *Patsy* one last victorious smile as he turned to go.

The priest walked himself through the door towards the exit as he heard cries of pain emanating from the cell behind him.

*****

As he walked out of the prison, the crisp autumn air brushed against his smile. He took the priest's collar off and shoved it into his jacket pocket as he strolled to the back of the prison parking lot, where a nondescript car with a moving container hitched behind it waited.

The man known to the press as *El Pinatero* drove down the highway with a cool wind through his hair. On the radio, the news announced the State had just put Patsy to death via the gas chamber. The news then announced the Cardinals had become World Series champions after beating the New York Yankees.

THE END